RETURN
OF THE
ENDER DRAGON

RETURN
OF THE
ENDER DRAGON

AN UNOFFICIAL OVERWORLD
HEROES ADVENTURE,
BOOK SIX

DANICA DAVIDSON

Sky Pony Press
New York

Copyright © 2018 by Danica Davidson

Minecraft® is a registered trademark of Notch Development AB.

The Minecraft game is copyright © Mojang AB.

This book is not authorized or sponsored by Microsoft Corp., Mojang AB, Notch Development AB or Scholastic Inc., or any other person or entity owning or controlling rights in the Minecraft name, trademark, or copyrights.

All rights reserved. No part of this book may be reproduced in any manner without the express written consent of the publisher, except in the case of brief excerpts in critical reviews or articles. All inquiries should be addressed to Sky Pony Press, 307 West 36th Street, 11th Floor, New York, NY 10018.

Sky Pony Press books may be purchased in bulk at special discounts for sales promotion, corporate gifts, fund-raising, or educational purposes. Special editions can also be created to specifications. For details, contact the Special Sales Department, Sky Pony Press, 307 West 36th Street, 11th Floor, New York, NY 10018 or info@skyhorsepublishing.com.

Sky Pony® is a registered trademark of Skyhorse Publishing, Inc.®, a Delaware corporation.

Minecraft® is a registered trademark of Notch Development AB. The Minecraft game is copyright © Mojang AB.

Visit our website at www.skyponypress.com.

10 9 8 7 6 5 4 3 2 1

Library of Congress Cataloging-in-Publication Data is available on file.

Cover design by Brian Peterson
Cover photo by Lordwhitebear

Hardcover ISBN: 978-1-5107-3355-8
Paperback ISBN: 978-1-5107-3354-1
Ebook ISBN: 978-1-5107-3356-5

Printed in Canada

RETURN
OF THE
ENDER DRAGON

CHAPTER 1

THE WORST HAD HAPPENED: THE ENDER DRAGON was free from her prison! And now she was towering right in front of me, my whole body cast in her shadow.

"Bow to me, Stevie," she commanded. Her black-as-night snout was inches from my face, her purple eyes burning like fire. "Bow to me or be defeated: those are your only choices."

It wasn't supposed to be like this! Thousands of years ago, the Overworld had almost been destroyed under the rule of the evil Ender Dragon. The monsters were her servants, and the humans were her victims. Then my famous ancestor, Steve Alexander, had imprisoned her in the End. If she ever escaped, it was up to my friends and me to stop her.

And we'd tried hard, so hard. We'd even managed to collect all the hidden Ender crystal shards Steve

1

Alexander had left for us. Those crystals were special and could make the ultimate weapon. But when we'd found the very last crystal, it was already too late. The Ender Dragon's Endermen guards had seized the latest crystal shard we'd found, and they'd stolen my friend, Maison. My last glimpse of Maison—my brave best friend who'd been with me through the most dangerous of our adventures—had been of her face frozen in terror.

Now I was standing outside my home in the Overworld, but the Ender Dragon's escape had caused a terrible change to come over the land. The sunny skies and green grass were gone, replaced by dark, churning clouds and screeching winds.

My dad, my cousin Alex, my Earth friends Yancy and Destiny, and Maison's mom were all standing with me. I kept waiting for Dad to tell me what to do. To say, "Get her with your sword, Stevie!" Or, "We'll ambush her."

Dad didn't say a thing. And I knew when Dad didn't say or do anything during a crisis, that was the scariest time of all: it meant there was nothing he *could* do.

What I needed was a plan. And some luck. I hoped that the Ender Dragon wouldn't think to look in my house, where the rest of the crystal shards were. While I stood there, a group of tall Endermen made their way over, followed by armed skeletons holding large swords.

I pulled together all the courage I could muster. "Where is Maison?" I shouted at the Ender Dragon.

"Yes, return my daughter!" Maison's mom cried. Her voice was almost lost in the wind.

"You think you can command me, pitiful humans?" the Ender Dragon hissed. "If you don't bow to me willingly, I will gladly force you."

I sucked in a breath. The Endermen and armed skeletons drew closer. They were obviously obeying the Ender Dragon. I didn't know what they'd do once they got within reach.

The Ender Dragon turned her eyes back on me. "You put up a worthy fight," she said. "I can see the blood of Steve Alexander running through your veins and the veins of your father and cousin. And the girl I took, that 'Maison' you speak of—I sense something in her blood as well."

Oh no! Maison's ancestor Maya was a woman from Earth who had helped Steve Alexander battle the dragon. I bet the Ender Dragon hated Maya too, and might take out her anger on Maison.

Then the Ender Dragon's snout prickled into a cruel smile, all fang and slyness. "Yes," she said. "You should be afraid for her, Stevie. Very afraid. Because if you don't answer my question now, Maison will be the one who suffers."

She made a signal with her tail. Just like that, the Endermen and armed skeletons came for us! Each Enderman teleported, appearing behind us and grabbing our hands, knocking away any weapons we were holding. Then they forced our hands behind our backs, clutching us by the wrists so we couldn't run.

My first thought was to kick behind me, but these evil servants weren't going to allow that, either. As an extra precaution, the armed skeletons stepped in front of us, holding their shiny swords inches from our faces. If I tried anything, I knew what would happen.

The Ender Dragon leaned her head into me. The heat of her breath was like standing next to a pool of lava. "Tell me where the other crystal shards are," she ordered.

I looked frantically at my dad. His face was stony and unreadable, and he wouldn't look at me. He couldn't tell me to give up on Maison, could he? However, giving her the rest of the Ender crystal shards was the same as admitting defeat. That's because those crystal shards held the key to making a weapon strong enough to stop the Ender Dragon.

Without meaning to, I must have glanced at my home. That was all the Ender Dragon needed.

"Tear the house to pieces!" she roared to her monster servants. "Don't stop until every shard has been found!"

CHAPTER 2

"**N**O!" I TRIED TO JOLT FORWARD AND COULDN'T. An Enderman held me in place. Other Endermen broke down the side of my house block by block. I pictured the iron box where we'd hidden the shards, and knew it couldn't be more than a matter of minutes before they found it. And then . . . and then . . .

I'm sorry, I'm so sorry. That was all I could think. *I failed. I failed everyone.*

"You're not going to get away with this!" raged Alex. "You know why?" Her temper was making her face so red it almost matched her hair. "Because you're right— we have Steve Alexander's blood in our veins! He beat you before, and we're going to do it again today and be back home in time for dinner! You just watch!"

I thought the Ender Dragon might go ballistic, but she just threw back her head and laughed. That evil laugh I'd heard before! Listening to it in real life sent a thunderous rumble through my insides.

"How sad that you believe those lies," the Ender Dragon said. "I know the Overworld now thinks of Steve Alexander as its greatest hero in history, a man who can make no mistakes and do no wrong. That's the danger in believing in heroes, little one. You will always be disappointed by a so-called hero's reality."

"Fat chance!" Alex shot back.

"So you really believe in him, then?" the Ender Dragon mocked. "Did you know it was he who first set me free upon the Overworld? That it was he who allowed me to become powerful by his side, so powerful that it was easy for me to take power?"

"That's not how it really happened," Alex replied sharply. "When he found you, you were locked up in chains with crystals in them, and you told him some sad lie to get him to release you. Then you just pretended to be his friend so you could steal power and betray him!"

Alex still wasn't done. "And then he defeated you and lived the rest of his life in peace while you were stuck in the End!" she finished triumphantly.

The dragon laughed. "How foolish you are," she said. "Lived out the rest of his life in peace? His story ended after we both fell through the End portal. Your hero didn't 'win'—I took him out when it was the two of us alone."

My heart instantly sank. No, it couldn't be true!

I had wanted so badly to believe there was a happy ending for him.

"Liar!" Alex spat.

"With only the two of us in the End, what did you think would happen?" the Ender Dragon demanded. "And when I was done taking care of him, I took his toolkit and threw it out into the void."

Alex was breathing so heavily I could hear it from where I was standing. But she refused to look down from the dragon's lava-spitting eyes. The Ender Dragon went on, "And the End is part of the Overworld now, isn't it? Can't you tell the veil between the realms has been torn? It will all be one land soon. My land."

An Enderman came out of the house. It swung its long arms and legs, making gestures to the dragon. Whatever it was trying to tell her now had her full attention. Just like that, the Ender Dragon went into a fury.

"What do you mean there are no crystal shards?" she screamed at it.

The Ender Dragon stormed over to the house, sticking her head through the hole in the wall. I saw my cat, Ossie, had hidden under some furniture but was untouched. The dragon forced furniture over and knocked through things, trying to find the shards. When her face came back out of the house, it was snarled up into the ugliest expression I'd ever seen on her.

"Where are the shards?" she shrieked at me.

"I – I don't know!" I stammered. It was the truth! "I thought they were in there!"

I felt a little bubble of hope starting to grow in my stomach. What was going on here? As long as the crystal shards didn't fall into her clutches, I didn't care where they were!

For a moment the Ender Dragon stared at us with barely contained fury. Then she struck her tail sharply against the ground, signaling her mob servants. The Endermen let go of our wrists and the armed skeletons backed up and pulled their swords away from us.

I expected the Ender Dragon to really let us have it then, not let us go! Why was she doing this?

Then I got my answer. My horrible, horrible answer.

Another Enderman appeared on the scene, holding Maison.

"Maison!" Maison's mom shouted, and tried to run for her. The armed skeletons held up their swords fence-like, blocking her.

"I offer you one chance," the Ender Dragon said. "Give me the crystal shards, and I will return your friend. If you do not bring me the rest of the crystal shards before nightfall, I will turn this girl into an Enderman."

"No," my voice broke out, barely above a whisper, even though I was panicking inside. Maison looked unhurt but wide-eyed, struggling to get loose from the Enderman's grip.

"As you all know, once she becomes an Enderman, she will soon lose her own mind," the Ender Dragon said. "She will become a servant of darkness, here only to make me happy."

"Don't give her the crystal shards!" Maison burst out. "If you do, I bet she'll turn all of us into Endermen! Into her servants!"

I found my voice then. "You can't do this!"

"What a pity," the Ender Dragon said, smiling. "I learned long ago the dangers in keeping a friendship." Her smile was much more evil than her voice ever sounded, because in the smile you could see how much she relished our suffering. "I told you, you will all bow to me in the end," she said. "Stevie, you know where to find me."

She snatched Maison up in her jaws, letting my best friend dangle there like a toy, and flew off into the dark skies.

CHAPTER 3

'D BEEN AN ENDERMAN BEFORE, AND I KNEW WHAT it meant. It'd felt like being trapped in darkness, without a will of your own. It was first turning into an Enderman that had allowed me to really feel the evil of the Ender Dragon and to let her into my head. But my friends had saved me in the nick of time, before I'd fully lost myself. I couldn't let the darkness win over Maison!

The mobs all turned away from us, as if we weren't interesting to them anymore. Were they really going to let us go?

Yes, because the Ender Dragon wanted those crystal shards more than anything else. As long as she didn't have them, we had a little power on our side.

"What do we do now?" It was Destiny whispering. I could barely hear her voice over the winds. Even so, her eyes were so etched with worry that I knew exactly what she was saying.

"We have to give the other crystal shards to the dragon to get Maison back!" Maison's mom said.

"We can't do that!" Yancy disagreed. "Maison was right. If we do that, we're all done for—including Maison."

"We're not going to leave my daughter in that dragon's grasp!" her mom insisted.

"We're going to do something," Yancy promised. "I'm saying we can't just give up those shards!"

"Where are those shards?" Destiny asked in a low voice, pushing her glasses up on her nose. "Are they lost?"

For the first time since the dragon left, Dad's face allowed itself to have an expression. It was relief.

"The crystal shards are safe," he said. "I hid them."

I was startled. "You hid them? Why?"

"I had a terrible sense of something bad coming our way," Dad said. "So I hid the crystals and went back to the portal to tell you. As I arrived, I saw the Endermen already in the house, and then all of you came through the portal."

That had all happened minutes ago, just before the dragon was freed.

"That's great, Uncle Steve!" Alex said. "Then we just get those shards, turn them into a weapon, and take out that dragon!"

"I don't think it will be that easy." Dad shook

his head. "We need all the shards in order to make a weapon strong enough to stop the Ender Dragon."

"We're at a stalemate, then?" Destiny asked. "Neither one of us has the upper hand?"

"Oh, I'd say *she* has the upper hand," Dad said. "Look at the Overworld—look at what she's done to it! Even without the other crystal shards, she's far more powerful than any of us."

"She's not going to get away with it!" Alex piped up. "And she's not going to get away with what she did to Steve Alexander, either!"

The mention of Steve Alexander sped up my heart. The Ender Dragon had treated him so cruelly, and they'd once been best friends. I wouldn't have believed it if I hadn't seen it with my own eyes. But the enchanted book Steve Alexander left behind had told us the whole back story, from Steve Alexander's unhappy childhood, to the quick time he was a hero in the Overworld for his mob fights with the Ender Dragon, then to his final battle to trap her in the End after her betrayal.

If she could do that to someone she might have actually cared about, what would she do to the rest of us?

"Follow me, kids," Dad said, leading us into the woods behind our house. The trees looked dark as coal, the winds tearing into their leaves. It looked like a haunted forest, not my own backyard. He dropped to his knees some distance out and began digging.

Under the dirt he pulled out the iron box—and the Ender crystal shards still safe inside. Just seeing that box helped me feel a little better.

"I don't know about this," Yancy said, rubbing up and down his arms as if he were cold. Blue, his pet parrot, was sitting on his left shoulder, and even he was quiet. Blue was always chirping and singing, so his silence added to the unsettling mood.

"What do you mean?" Alex demanded.

"She's offering us too nice of a bargain," Yancy said.

"She's threatening to turn our friend into a mindless Enderman!" Alex exploded, outraged by what he said. "That's not a nice bargain!"

"No, but look at the fact that she's bargaining with us at all," Yancy said. "And the fact her servants left us alone. She could have done whatever she wanted to us back there. She's scared she's not going to get those shards."

"Yancy is right," Dad said gruffly, staring off into the cold, haunted trees. There was a mist settling through the land, almost purple in color, like the purple of the End. Or of the Ender Dragon's eyes. "We have some advantage over her, and she knows that. But she also knows she has the upper hand. We have no choice but to give her the shards."

"What?" Yancy said. "No, that's not what I said! I said we can't give her the shards! We have to think of something else!"

Dad turned his eyes away from the forest and

stared at Yancy instead. "Then what do you suggest? What would you do in that *Minecraft* game of yours?"

"I . . . I . . ." Yancy said.

"We can use some kind of codes to outsmart her," Destiny said. "Like we did with Herobrine." She pulled out her cell phone and began tapping on it with her thumb. A moment later, her whole face crumpled. "My phone won't turn on! It's not working here!"

"Maybe it's this weather," Yancy said darkly.

"See," Alex shot to Yancy. "I told you that your fancy old 'technology' isn't that great. It can just blow up when you need it most." She made a sound of TNT exploding to further prove her point. Yancy glared at her. He and Alex had been picking little fights about technology for a while, and this time it looked like Alex won.

"We don't need any tech to stop the Ender Dragon," Alex said.

"No, we need a miracle," Yancy said.

"We need Steve Alexander." I didn't realize the words were out of my mouth until I saw everyone was looking at me. My voice sounded as low and depressed as I felt. "He would come up with something clever."

"Stevie, Steve Alexander is gone." This was Maison's mom talking. Her eyes were red from trying not to cry, and I could tell she wanted nothing more than to run after the Ender Dragon until she caught up and got her daughter back. "I don't know much about your world, but I know enough that's been passed down in my family, ever since Maya lived. You can't always look to other people to get you out of bad situations. You have to find your own courage."

"She's right," Dad said.

Ossie the cat slunk slowly over to us, glancing around. She looked as startled as the rest of us. Destiny picked her up and held her close.

"There's something else that bothers me," Yancy said. "What did she mean when she said, 'Stevie, you know where to find me'? Stevie, do you have any idea? Uh, Stevie?"

I was only half-listening because something had distracted me. At first I thought I heard the sound of a strange new monster. As the sound grew louder, I recognized it, and it wasn't anything like the sound a monster would make.

In the purple mist, framed by the black of the twisted trees, I saw the outline of a dog, its eyes shining in my direction. The dog raised its head and bayed toward the sky.

I know that dog, I thought in the back of my mind. And I began to follow it.

CHAPTER 4

I WAS IN A TRANCE, LIKE WHEN STEVE ALEXANDER helped me during our clash in the ocean monument, two missions ago. The dark forest fell behind me like a backdrop, and all I could think about was this dog.

When the dog saw me coming, he turned and trotted in the other direction. His white fur looked slightly pink in all the purple lighting, and his red collar jangled as he moved.

While I walked, I uncovered more and more images of the End. Through the fog I saw violet-colored purpur blocks and white islands. This must be what the Ender Dragon meant when she said that the veil between the realms had been torn. No, they weren't one and the same. But here I was stepping over a piece of purpur block that had appeared in the mist or turning my head to see a purple skyscraper jutting over the trees.

"Stevie!" I heard Dad call. "Come back!"

I heard Yancy shout, "Stevie, it's not time to go into one of your little sleepwalking modes! You're scaring us!"

Oh, I wasn't sleepwalking. Even though I didn't feel quite there, I was totally awake.

Every once in a while the dog glanced back over his shoulder to make sure I was still following him. He was leading me deeper into the End, into more and more purple. At this point we shouldn't have been far from my home, but I didn't recognize anything I was seeing.

"It's an End city!" I heard Destiny exclaim as they passed by the purple skyscraper too.

"An End city?" repeated Maison's mom. "I don't think I like the sound of that."

I heard Yancy explain, "In the *Minecraft* game, you can find these big purple cities in the End. So the Ender Dragon must have . . ."

I stopped moving. Why was there no more ground right in front of me? I peered over it, and saw nothing but empty blackness underneath. A wave of dizziness hit my head and I pulled back. An End island. This land had been turned into an End island!

The dog was toward my left, trying to draw me along. He didn't want me to go to the edge of the island, where nothing awaited me except for a fall down into . . . into what? Into the void.

I followed the dog up a little hill. When I got to the top of it, I could look through the haze and see several white islands floating in the distance, looking entrancing and otherworldly. For a second they caught my attention so much I lost my footing.

"Stevie!" Dad cried as I took a spill.

I thumped down the little hill, landing on the bottom in a stupor. Ugh. I pulled myself back up and sat there for a second, letting my head stop spinning. The dog licked my hand and a man's voice breathed in gratitude, "Thank you, Wolf. You brought him."

Wolf?

My head flew back up. The purple was there like a cloud, and in the middle of it was a small prison cell. It glinted in the weak light like silver fangs, trapping a single man inside of it. The man was clutching the bars of the cell, trying to break it.

"No way," I gasped.

Was I dreaming? Was I back in a memory from the enchanted book?

No. I stood up and walked over to the cell, and the man there was breathing and as real as I was. I looked at his dark hair, his square beard. I remembered that voice.

"It can't be you!" I said, the trance breaking. "Steve Alexander!"

CHAPTER 5

THERE WAS THE GREATEST MAN THE OVERWORLD had ever known, locked up behind bars. The others were coming down the hill to join me, calling out my name. As soon as they reached me, I heard their intakes of breath. They couldn't believe what they were seeing, either. Destiny was still holding Ossie, keeping her safe in her arms.

"But . . . but . . ." I stammered. I didn't know how to say it nicely, so it just came out bluntly, "How are you still alive?"

"Stevie!" Dad barked. I knew he wouldn't like how I said it. Trying to make up for me, Dad quickly said, "Steve Alexander, it is an honor. We'll get you out of there right away."

Dad took his diamond sword and struck the lock of the cell. Nothing! There was a screeching noise and a sputter of sparks, and that was it.

"No normal sword will work on this," Steve Alexander said. "She made sure of that."

We didn't need to ask who "she" was. We all knew.

"Let me try!" Alex gleefully offered, pulling back her arrows. Several arrows hit the lock, one right after another, and they also had no effect. Alex looked outraged. I knew she had wanted to save Steve Alexander herself, so that she could show off.

"Don't worry," Steve Alexander said. "You have the crystal shards. I felt you collect them all . . ."

He stopped, seeing our faces. A slow horror went over his own face.

"How much of the crystal did she get?" he quickly demanded.

"Just one shard," I said. "We have the rest." I hoped that counted for something. Steve Alexander's face went from horrified to grim, so I guessed it didn't count for much.

"Hand me one of the crystal shards," Steve Alexander said. He tried to reach one hand out of the bars to help. His hand couldn't quite get out. When the Ender Dragon had trapped him there, she'd made sure to make bars just slightly smaller than his hands.

Wordlessly, Dad brought out the other crystal shards. Despite all the purple mist around, the purple of the crystals still burned much brighter. He struck the lock and the bars parted, releasing the prisoner.

I was ready for Steve Alexander to leap courageously out of the cell, prepared to battle. Prepared to take on the Ender Dragon, to rescue Maison, to make everything better. I think my heart dropped when I watched him slowly stumble out, as if he hadn't used his legs in a long time. His shoulders were a little stooped. He looked exhausted.

This didn't look like any sort of a hero. Where was the man who'd valiantly forced the dragon into the End? Where was the brave man in the statues, the hero of the Overworld we'd all been taught about since we were little? This was just an ordinary man, with sloped shoulders and a grimace on his face.

Alex didn't feel any of the disappointment I did. As soon as Steve Alexander was out, she and Wolf both jumped on him, Wolf to lick him and Alex to hug him.

"I knew that mean old dragon couldn't defeat you!" she said. "We'll have no problem defeating her today. And we'll be home in time for dinner!"

Dad introduced himself and all of us, but Steve Alexander looked lost in thought.

"Not having the last crystal is very serious," my ancestor said, thinking hard. "I thought I sensed something bad happen. Where is the last girl, Maya's descendant?"

Maison's mom let out a long moan.

Steve Alexander stared at us in horror. "Don't tell me Jean got her!"

Jean. That was the Ender Dragon's old name, back before her betrayal.

"The dragon said we could have Maison back if

we give over the rest of the shards," Dad said. "I don't think we have much choice here."

"There's always a choice," Steve Alexander said. "Hold on, let me think."

He turned away from us, his hand to his chin. Something stirred on his back, like feathers.

"What is that?" I blurted out, confused.

"Stevie!" Dad snapped. What he meant was: stop talking and let Steve Alexander think!

Steve Alexander sighed and turned back. "No, it's all right," he said. "I owe you some answers before we continue. The reason I'm still alive is very simple: time moves differently in the End and the Overworld. Thousands of years for you was just a few years for me."

"Talk about a fountain of youth," Yancy said dryly. "But I guess it makes sense if time's different in the End. There's no day or night there."

Just darkness, I thought. And shivered.

"After I pushed Jean into the End," Steve Alexander went on, "I knew I was no longer any match for her. I quickly stole away, so that she didn't know where I was in this new land. Then I journeyed around the End the best I could, given that it's mostly made up of islands over a void. Eventually, I found a ship and inside of it were a pair of wings."

"Those are wings?" I said, amazed. They looked pretty ratty now, as if they could never fly.

"Yes," Steve Alexander said. "I call them 'elytra.' I began flying around the End, collecting supplies. I even began making a cell to put Jean in. Then one day, it was too late. Jean found me while I was flying, and broke my wings. She laughed at me, saying, 'You want to fly like a dragon? I'll clip your wings and send you straight back to the ground.'"

"And then what?" I cried.

"She took the cell I'd created, made it smaller and threw me in," he said. "Then she tossed my toolkit—where I had all the supplies I'd ever made—out into the void. All I could do was sit and wait. Thank goodness I had Wolf here to keep me company. He's always been a loyal companion."

He patted the dog on the head. Wolf's tongue lolled happily and he barked.

"Then I sensed Jean beginning to make her plans for escape," Steve Alexander said. "I could sense Stevie and Alex at first, and then I could sense Maya's descendant. Next I began to sense that they'd brought friends from Earth to help them." He nodded toward Yancy and Destiny in acknowledgment. "I knew it would fall to them to stop her. I tried to speak out whenever I could, but Jean kept me under close watch much of the time."

"It's okay now, though!" I said quickly. "We have most of the crystal shards, and we have you!" Tired or not, I had no doubt that Steve Alexander was just what we needed!

Out of the darkness behind us, I heard familiar voices shouting, "Help! Help! Is anyone out there?"

CHAPTER 6

WE ALL RAN TOWARD THE VOICES, EVEN Steve Alexander. I saw he was starting to get his footing back. Maybe he just needed more time moving around to get like normal again.

On top of the hill I saw two figures stumbling through the violet mists. Their steps were so unsteady it made me think I was looking at zombies. But then I heard the voice shout, "Help! Help!" again.

It was the village blacksmith, along with the village librarian. What were they doing all the way out here?

"Blacksmith! Librarian!" Dad called. "We're over here!"

"Thank goodness we found you, Steve!" exclaimed the blacksmith. Both men began stumbling closer toward us. "The village is . . . the village is . . ."

He choked on the words as if he couldn't bring himself to say them. Dad was next to them in an instant, demanding, "What about the village? Are you hurt?"

"No, not hurt," the blacksmith gasped. "We managed to get away. All those storms started whipping up earlier, and then . . ."

"A dark shadow fell over the whole village!" the librarian burst out. "And a dragon flew over it!"

"We were overrun," the blacksmith said. "Monsters came out of all corners of the Overworld. Mostly it was Endermen and armed skeletons, but there were zombies and creepers too! The armored skeletons surrounded the village like a siege, so that no one could get in or out. And then the Endermen started moving from house to house. Every household was given two choices: bow to the dragon, or become an Enderman."

"No!" I exclaimed.

"What do you mean, given two choices?" Dad asked. "Endermen can't talk!"

"They can't," the blacksmith agreed. "But she can." He pointed toward the sky. He didn't have to say another word.

"We could hear her voice in our heads!" the librarian said, shuddering. "She said the same thing was happening to every village in the Overworld!"

"What did the people do?" Dad wanted to know.

"At first, they tried to fight," the blacksmith said. "It didn't take them long to see it did no good. A few tried to make an escape and were caught by the armed skeletons. They were immediately handed over to the Endermen for transformation. Then the people began refusing, thinking this could stall time. It didn't. They were immediately transformed into Endermen too. Finally some people started falling to their knees and singing praises of the dragon. They were given weapons."

"I knew it!" Yancy said darkly. "She's saving Maison for us, but she's just going to treat us all the same in the end!"

"How did you escape?" Dad asked.

"The only way we knew how," the blacksmith said. "We went into some mines and tunneled our way out of the village. When we were beyond the village gates, we dug back to the surface and went running for you. Then we got lost in this fog . . ."

"It's even worse than I feared," said a voice from behind us. Steve Alexander stepped forward, his head down. "Even with that one crystal shard, it's raised her power immensely. It won't take her very long to transform every citizen of the Overworld into an Enderman or a mindless servant."

"Either way, it's the same results," Yancy remarked bitterly. "Servitude to the Ender Dragon."

"We have to seek her out," Steve Alexander said, pacing angrily. "We have to put a stop to this."

I bit my tongue, a sour feeling of guilt spreading all over me. If only we had taken better care of all the crystals, we wouldn't be in this mess!

"Don't worry about us!" came a bright voice. It was Alex of course, beaming and holding her arrows. "We're the Overworld Heroes task force. We were made to stop the dragon."

"I have no weapons," Steve Alexander began. "And there isn't time for me to make more."

"Take this," said the blacksmith, handing over a diamond sword. "I got it away from a man who promised to follow the dragon. I didn't think he deserved it . . ."

"Thank you," Steve Alexander said, taking back the sword. Was that a little smile on his face? "It's good to know that diamond swords are still in use." I knew he was thinking about the fact he'd invented them. I wondered how different the world must be if you've been away from it for thousands of years, and what would stick out to you.

"If the Ender Dragon is going after villages, that should mean people in the countryside are relatively safe . . . for now," Dad said to the blacksmith and the librarian. "You should try to find others in the countryside and see if you can take back any of the villages."

"But what about you?" the blacksmith cried.

Steve Alexander held his new diamond sword up to the sky and watched how it glinted, even in this bad lighting. "What about us?" he said. "We're going dragon hunting."

CHAPTER 7

WE LEFT THE BLACKSMITH AND LIBRARIAN behind, going deeper into the purple fog, out past where Steve Alexander had been locked up. I walked behind him, totally in awe. Yes, he was definitely getting his footing back, and the more he walked, the more I could see the hero of centuries ago. We came to the end of a white island and Steve Alexander knelt down and studied below it.

"I think I know where she went," he said. "During our time in here, she collected her own set of Ender crystals. She didn't use them to make a weapon. Instead, she used their natural healing abilities and she set them all up on another island, so that she can sit in the middle of the crystals."

"That's just like in the game!" Yancy said. "You have to take out all those health crystals before you can finish the Ender Dragon."

"Game?" Steve Alexander repeated, confused.

"Never mind him," Dad quickly said. He found Yancy calling our world "a game" to be offensive, and he probably figured Steve Alexander did too. Standing in front of a living legend, I think we all wanted to be careful how we came across to him. You didn't want to look stupid in front of someone like Steve Alexander.

"No, explain it to me," Steve Alexander said, turning to Yancy and Destiny. "I recognize you as being people from Earth, but your clothing and mannerisms are strange to me."

"Well, times have changed since you were last at Earth," Yancy said. "You missed some things, like, oh, the printing press, electricity, the Internet . . . yeah, okay, so you've missed a lot of things."

"Are any of these things weapons?" Steve Alexander asked.

"I . . . guess they could be used as weapons," Yancy said, thinking over it. "But none of them were meant to be used as weapons. Here." He took out his phone and showed it to Steve Alexander.

Steve Alexander turned the phone this way and that, fascinated. "How does it work?"

"It lets you talk to people miles away!" Yancy answered. "It lets you email people, text people, play games like *Minecraft*. Lots of people know about your world now, only they don't know it's a real world, and they think it's a game. That's what I was talking about earlier. They're always coming out with new phones to make life better and easier!"

"I just see a black screen," Steve Alexander said.

"Well, it isn't working now," Yancy admitted, embarrassed and drooping. "But if we were on Earth, I could show you all sorts of things!"

"Does your phone have the power to stop a dragon?" Steve Alexander asked. "Does it put food on your table? Does it make you a better person?"

"Well . . . uh," was all Yancy could say.

"Then it is of no use to us now," Steve Alexander said, handing the phone back.

"I guess it's all about how you decide to use it," Yancy said. Then he added under his breath, "When it has reception."

"Maya did not have all these inventions," Steve Alexander said. "She had what she needed: smarts and bravery."

"We have that too," Destiny said, sounding a little hurt. "We've defeated lots of mobs."

"We need a way to get to the other islands," Steve Alexander said, looking back out at the void.

"You can fix those wings with an anvil and some leather," Yancy said, eyeing the ruffled feathers running down Steve Alexander's back. "Then you can fly."

"And leave you behind?" Steve Alexander said. "No, we need all of us for this. What we need is another ship, and you can find them on some of these End islands. The ship will allow us to cross the void."

"Aye, aye!" Yancy said. I didn't want to tell Yancy this, but I thought Steve Alexander had a point that phones weren't the fix-it-alls Earth people made them out to be. When I was on Earth, I thought a lot of people were too attached to their phones. They said it helped them connect to other people, which I thought was neat. But if they used it in place of seeing people face to face, I thought it more did the opposite a lot of the time.

Everyone spread out on the foggy island, looking for a hidden ship. Everyone except for Steve Alexander and me. He was still looking out over the void like looking out at sea, and he had a wistful, sad expression on his face. What was he thinking? I decided I better say something.

"We're really glad you're here," I started. "You were always so helpful when you'd give me clues on my missions." I decided not to point out that he often didn't give me clues and left me to figure things out on my own. When he'd done that, I'd usually complained about it at the time. But afterward I kept feeling as if I had grown from the experience, even though I hated the experience whenever I was going through it.

Steve Alexander turned back from the void and looked at me. The wind kept moving the feathers on his back, making them almost look like an old cape that'd grown tattered and worn.

Now that we were alone again and he was looking at me, I started to feel self-conscious and embarrassed. The fact he wasn't talking didn't help any. It just made me want to talk more to fill in the silence. But the more I talked, the dumber I began to feel.

"I've looked up to you since I was little," I said. "My dad always told me we were related to you, and I didn't believe him until recently. Now I know the truth. I think what you did to help the Overworld is really, really amazing."

I wanted to wince at myself. Now Steve Alexander was staring at me as if he didn't know what I was talking about. I thought people were supposed to like hearing praise about themselves. I knew I always liked it when people said good things about me.

So I quickly added, "You're my hero."

He cringed. Why did he cringe? My mouth went dry.

Then he said, "Look, Stevie, part of growing up is facing new things. I'm not your hero or anyone else's."

"Wh-what do you mean?" I faltered.

"People get called 'heroes' one day, and something else the next. No person can fit the bill of a perfect 'hero' because no person is that good. The idea of a hero is a dangerous one. I used to think Jean was my hero, because she saved me from my loneliness and then rode into battle with me each night to fight the mobs. The people of the world were cruel, but Jean was just. Think what a lesson I had to learn when I realized Jean had never been a hero."

"That's just one example!" I said. "And even if you're not perfect, you're good!"

Even as he said it, I hated to say I saw the points he was making. Sometimes people had called me a hero for saving the Overworld. Part of me really loved hearing that, and part of me didn't feel comfortable with it. Why? Because I knew what I was like. I was a kid who fell off pigs while riding them or got annoyed with Dad or forgot something I was supposed to do. Those didn't sound like things heroes did. So when people called me a hero, it felt like they believed in a perfect side of me that didn't exist, and it would only be so long before they saw the real Stevie, the Stevie who often fell short.

"I do good actions when I can," Steve Alexander said. "I think that's just called behaving decently. I don't call that being a hero."

I thought back on the villagers who'd given over to the Ender Dragon instead of fighting. They hadn't tried to do a good action . . . but was that just because they didn't have the choice? Or they felt they didn't have the choice? The blacksmith and librarian had made it out of the village without turning, so there were possible escapes that I guessed other people hadn't considered.

"No one else stood up to the Ender Dragon when she rose to power in the past," I pointed out. "Only you did."

"That's not being a hero, Stevie," he said. "I think it more says something about how much people will avoid anything unpleasant unless they have to."

He started to turn away, to leave me with my thoughts.

"Wait," I called out.

He stopped and turned back. "What is it?"

"Why do you still call her Jean?" I asked. "She calls herself the Ender Dragon. That's what we all call her. She hasn't been Jean since . . ."

I stopped. This time when there was silence, I didn't feel a need to fill it. Because even though he didn't say a word to me, I thought I saw the answer in his eyes. He called her Jean because a part of him couldn't let go of the friend he'd had. A part of him still wanted desperately for her to be Jean, somewhere inside of her.

And then Steve Alexander turned and walked into the purple fog, joining the others in the search for the ship. The only sound was the wind.

That's the danger in believing in heroes, little one. You will always be disappointed by a so-called hero's reality.

The memory of the Ender Dragon's words rang in my mind. Thousands of years had let us build Steve Alexander up in our minds without ever knowing the man. Here I'd thought that once we'd released him, he would have immediately taken charge. I could take a back seat to him and not feel scared, and with his leadership we'd quickly take out the Ender Dragon and get Maison back to safety.

And what were we? The Overworld Heroes task force? That felt like such a joke right now.

Maison, we're coming for you, I thought. Even if we can't count on Steve Alexander like I thought we could.

If he refused to see how great he could be, I could still rise above that. I would stop looking for confidence in Steve Alexander and find it elsewhere. Maison's life and the lives of everyone in the Overworld depended on it.

I started to walk through the fog, looking for any signs of a ship. Even as I looked, I couldn't get Steve Alexander's face or voice out of my mind.

My first thought, when I'd seen him stumble out of the cell, had been right. The Steve Alexander of legend was the hero we could all relate to. And the Steve Alexander of reality was a shaken, worn-out man. He was a man who had lost his best friend, had suffered the worst betrayal, and had been locked away. A man whose only possession was a broken pair of wings that could no longer fly.

CHAPTER 8

AN EXCITED YELL RIPPED ME OUT OF MY thoughts.

"A ship! A ship!" Yancy was shouting. "I found us a ship!"

I ran toward his voice, passing by more mysterious purple buildings. The towers jutted out of the fog like the moon appearing from out of the clouds. Banners fluttered on top of buildings. Nothing about this landscape felt quite real. And when I skittered over to where Yancy was standing, the ship just made it all more dreamlike.

I'd gone boating with Dad plenty of times. We always made the boats ourselves out of wood and they would fit a few people at most.

By comparison, this ship could have probably held a hundred people comfortably. Maybe more. It had a long deck, a little cabin in the middle you could walk into, and a tall line for a mast. There was even a crow's hatch you could get to if you walked up some stairs. I didn't know the names for all the parts of a ship, but I recognized this type of ship as one they also have on Earth. Or had. Maison had shown me pictures of ships like this, and she said they were used a few hundred years ago.

I was the first to reach Yancy, who was beaming in pride over the ship. A moment later Alex arrived and she let out a whoop.

"It's huge!" she said. "Now that's the way to travel!"

Dad and Maison's mom joined us right then, followed by Destiny a few seconds later.

"That's not even the best part," Yancy said, still beaming. "Look at it! Don't you know what it looks like?"

We all stared at him blankly.

Yancy was so excited he could barely contain it. "It looks like a pirate ship! An old-timey pirate ship for the pirates in old books!"

We all stared blankly at him. Then I understood and groaned. That Yancy! Even when things were at their worst he could find something amusing to him. (It usually wasn't so amusing to the rest of us.) And ever since he tamed his parrot Blue he'd been going on about pirate this and pirate that. "Don't I look like a pirate?" he'd say, pointing to the bird on his shoulder. Or, "Argh, matey, we're here to look for treasure!" while we were getting ready for another crystal mission.

Everyone except Yancy thought the whole pirate thing had gotten old.

"How do we get onboard?" I asked. Yancy frowned. I knew he'd wanted me to say something about pirates, but I wanted to get down to business!

You see, there was something different about this ship, and I don't just mean its size or its purple color. It was floating off the ground, out of our reach. We couldn't climb up to it, and we couldn't jump to it, either. I didn't know what was keeping it afloat, so I guessed it was enchantments from the End.

Steve Alexander stepped out of the fog, surveying the ship. "Good job!" he told Yancy. "Now I . . ." His hand went to where he used to keep his toolkit. Of course there wasn't anything there, and that made his face cloud over.

"Normally I would teleport there using an Ender pearl," he said. "Unfortunately . . ."

"No problem!" Alex said. "We can build a bridge there using end stone bricks!"

"Good thinking," Steve Alexander said.

There were plenty of end stone bricks around, and we all grabbed them and built ourselves a little bridge up into the ship. With the whole group of us working, it didn't take long. I tried not to look down.

"Last one in is a rotten egg!" Alex called. She hopped onto the deck while the rest of us followed, then quickly moved around, exploring it.

And she wasn't the only one excited to be onboard.

"Shiver me timbers!" Yancy crowed when he got on the deck. "This here be a fine pirate ship!"

I didn't understand half of that. Blue chirped happily.

"Look at the front of the ship!" Alex called gleefully, peering over the edge.

"I've heard of pirate ships having mermaid figureheads at the bows," Destiny said, setting Ossie safely down on the deck. Ossie began to sniff and check out her surroundings. "Not dragons."

Dragons? I peeked over the front end of the ship. At first all I saw was the empty, dizzy drop below, where a person could fall and fall and fall and never stop falling. That made me not want to lean too far over it. I pulled back a little, so that only the top of my head was peeking over. I looked down and saw the snarling face of a dragon!

I leapt back to safety, heart pounding. Laughter rang out behind me, and it was from Alex.

"Relax, Stevie," she said. "It's not real. In fact . . ."

Before I could tell her she was crazy, Alex jumped over the front of the ship.

"Alex, no!" I cried, getting back up. I peeked over the front edge of the ship again. Alex was holding on to the ship, balancing herself to get the dragon head. She took blocks out of her toolkit to brace around the head, allowing her to get it. The face kept snarling at her as if it would bite, but she was correct: it wasn't real.

"Got it!" Alex said, waving the dragon head around before dropping it triumphantly in her toolkit. "I wonder what I can make using this."

"Alex, this isn't the time," Dad shouted down to her, frowning.

"But Uncle Steve!" Alex replied. "How often do you get to take home a dragon head? Hopefully we'll get two today, if you know what I mean!"

Steve Alexander was nearby and he made a disgusted sound, like he didn't care for what Alex said. I wanted to say something, but he had already turned away, his winged back to me. I wondered why he didn't just get rid of those wings if they weren't working.

Wait a second. I thought back. Didn't he say he found those wings in a ship? Did that mean this ship might also have its own pair of wings?

Leaving Dad and Alex to argue in the background, I headed toward the little cabin below deck. There was an opening that led down there, and a little set of stairs. In the cabin I saw a brewing stand with two potions on it. I picked the potions up to investigate. They were both Potions of Healing, which could come in useful.

There was another stairway going farther down into the belly of the ship. No one else had followed me, and I could hear them all making a fuss onboard. Alex was still defending her dragon head, Dad was telling her we had to get to business, and Yancy was trying to get Blue to say, "Shiver me timbers!" Whatever that meant. I wondered what Steve Alexander thought of us. He probably wasn't all that impressed.

Down the stairway I went, into the last room. This room was much longer than the last room, though it wasn't very wide. In the far corner I saw two chests between a purple block and . . . and . . .

A pair of gray wings hanging on the wall.

I couldn't believe my luck! I went straight for the pair of wings, not even thinking about what great treasures might be hidden in the chests. After seeing Steve Alexander's tattered wings, this pair looked so pure and perfect, never used.

But as soon as I stepped forward and reached out, the purple block split in two and a monster was after me.

CHAPTER 9

NEVER SAW IT COMING! ONE SECOND IT WAS JUST AN-
other purple block, like a million other purple blocks
I'd seen in the End city. Then it split down the middle
and a face was staring at me from inside it, like the cen-
ter of a seashell. It was just a square little floating head,
with two eyes and a mouth—it looked pretty harmless.
It could be a pet or an animal to keep on a farm. Then
it opened its mouth and shot a jagged projectile at me.

I jumped to the side, trying to dodge it! At the
same time, I automatically slashed out at the creature
with my diamond sword. It was instinct. But the shell
shut, making it look like a regular block again. That
wasn't even the worst part. The projectile followed me,
going off its path to make sure it hit!

I grunted from the brunt of it, then felt my feet lift
off the ground. Wait, what was happening? I didn't
have the wings, so why was I flying?

Actually, flying wasn't the right word. I was float-ing, and it wasn't my choice. Something in the projec-tile had done this!

"Help!" I called. "Help!"

As if it heard me, the purple block popped back open and the little square creature shot another pro-jectile my way. I tried to stop it with my sword and couldn't. The projectile crashed into me, and then I floated farther up into the air. I hit against the ceiling, floating there like a ghost!

"HELLLPPP!" I shouted, louder. I tried to move and it was like awkwardly swimming through air. The whole back part of me was sticking against the ceiling.

All the fussy voices upstairs stopped bickering and I heard their footsteps as everyone ran down below. Steve Alexander and Wolf were the first to make it. Wolf came barreling across the room, and when the creature opened its shell to blast me again, the dog pounced on it and took it out. The creature was gone, but I was still floating against the ceiling!

Dad came into the room, did a quick look around, then spied me. "Stevie!" he hollered. "Stop playing around! First Alex and now you!"

Alex, Yancy, Destiny, and Maison's mom were down there next. Ossie peeked her head through Destiny's legs, wanting to see what the commotion was about.

"Whoa!" Alex said, thrilled. "How'd you do that, Stevie? I want to do it too!"

"I can't get down," I told Dad, really embarrassed. I

found I could kind of slide around on the ceiling, and that was it.

"What did you touch?" Dad asked suspiciously.

"I know what happened here," Steve Alexander said, looking unfazed. "Stevie met a shulker, a little mob that hides in purple blocks and shoots projectiles. You just find them in End cities, and they put the Levitation effect on you."

"Is it awesome up there, Stevie?" Alex called up.

I wouldn't say it was awesome. I really wanted back down! Not having control over gravity was freaking me out.

"It's easily fixed," Steve Alexander said, still calm. "I've dealt with a few of them myself. Just give him some milk to drink."

Dad reached into his toolkit and tossed me up a glass of milk. "We shouldn't have to waste milk on things like this!" he told me. In the Overworld, milk healed us and we only had so much on hand, so I knew we had to be careful.

"Don't be too hard on the boy," Steve Alexander said as I caught the milk and began drinking. "It could be worse. He could be floating into space now. It's a good thing he's indoors."

Dad paled. "In space?"

"Yes," Steve Alexander said. "Eventually the Levitation device will lose its power, and then he'd plummet back to the ground from wherever he was."

That happened anyway. After I'd swallowed the milk, gravity came back in a rush and I fell straight to the floor, groaning on impact. Here I was, trying to be smart and get myself a pair of wings while the others were fussing. And all I'd done was make myself look bad and waste some milk!

"Keep your eyes peeled for shulkers," Steve Alexander said, looking down at me. It would have been nicer if he'd helped me back up. I slowly pulled myself to my feet. "You might run into some more."

"Hey, it's not all bad," Yancy said. "Stevie also found treasure!"

He popped open the chests, revealing glowing layers of gold and other amazing finds. "Here's some pirate booty!" he said to Blue. Blue whistled and ruffled his feathers happily.

"Some rare finds can be discovered in End ships' chests," Steve Alexander said, pushing his way through to also check out the chests. "Are there any good weapons there?"

"Weapons?" Yancy said, digging his hands through gold. "No, I don't see any weapons."

Alex dug into the other chest. "No, nothing here, either."

Steve Alexander seemed to be thinking.

Still feeling a little weird from my floating adventure, I made my way back over. I wasn't interested in the chests. My eyes were still on the wings. I carefully pulled them down from the wall.

"Elytra," Steve Alexander said, nodding his approval. "Hold on to those, Stevie."

"I think we're missing the point here," Maison's mom said, frowning. "We can't be looking at gold or wings when we have to get Maison back!"

Here the rest of us were, getting distracted. Especially Yancy with his dumb pirate stuff. But Maison's mom had haunted eyes. Not having Maison back had to be eating away at her, the way I could feel it eating away at me. This weekend was Maison's birthday, and I was still trying to figure out what I was going to give her. It had to be something special. But if we couldn't get her back . . .

"Maison is brave," Yancy said, closing the chest. "She's not going to let that dragon push her around."

"She's a little girl against a huge dragon!" Maison's mom argued, horrified. "As it is, we have sulk—shulk— whatever that thing was, jumping out of blocks! What can be happening to Maison now?"

"Maison's great at *Minecraft* . . ." Destiny began.

"No!" her mom shouted. "This is not normal. I know we have a family history that dates back to Steve Alexander. I know my ancestor Maya fought monsters before. But she was an adult and knew what she was getting into. We need to hurry."

Yancy, Destiny, and Alex looked properly shamed. I agreed with Maison's mom, that we needed to hurry. (And I could use something to get us to stop thinking about me floating.)

"I know the island Jean is on," Steve Alexander said. "Unfortunately, with the veil between the Overworld and the End torn the way it is, pieces of land are moving and everything is out of whack. I don't know how to get there from here."

The look Maison's mom got on her face then was awful. It was like all the humanity melted off it, and it was a mask that showed nothing but horror.

"I know where they are," I said.

CHAPTER 10

"I CAN FEEL HER," I SAID. "HER EVIL PRESENCE." I SHUT my eyes, trying to see where she was. I tried to feel Maison too. If I felt Maison's presence with the Ender Dragon's, I might be able to tell somehow if she were hurt.

But I couldn't feel Maison, and I couldn't see anything, try as I might. All I felt was that deep, leaden feeling in my stomach, like a feeling of having ice water thrown on you.

"I can lead us there!" I said, hurrying up the steps, back onto the deck. I ran to the hull and felt the wind whipping against my face. Across from me was a black stretch of eternity, with a few small white islands floating in the distance.

"That way." I pointed.

"Aye, aye, captain," Yancy said, turning the ship. I felt the floor beneath me shift as the creaking ship turned in the right direction and began to move.

Something touched my leg and I looked down. It was Wolf, pawing at me gently. When I reached down to pet him, he happily leaned his head into the pet and wagged his tail. It felt like he was trying to encourage me. No wonder he had been such a great companion to Steve Alexander, especially when he was in imprisoned in the End. It was funny, how young Steve Alexander had said that he was lonely so much. He meant he was hungry for human company, and I got that. But he'd never really been alone, because Wolf had been there to love him the whole time.

As we sailed deeper into the darkness, I concentrated on feeling the Ender Dragon's evil power. I'd hated the connection I'd had with her ever since I'd turned into an Enderman and she'd first gotten into my head. Now it was going to have to be that connection that got us to her, so that we could battle.

Could we actually win?

I heard Steve Alexander muttering and groaning. What was going on? I turned back and saw he was down in the cabin, at the brewing stand. He was trying to use the brewing stand as a crafting table. He'd laid the crystal shards out and was attempting to make something of them. Dad was next to him, pulling out different items from his toolkit to see if Steve Alexander had any ideas.

"What about my diamond pickaxe?" Dad asked. "Surely you can add that to the crystal shards and make it a superior weapon."

Steve Alexander shook his head. "It wouldn't be the same. I really need all those crystal shards to do anything."

Alex pulled her dragon's head out of her toolkit. "Can you use this?"

Steve Alexander shook his head. From where he was steering the ship, Yancy called, "Alex, you just pulled that out to show it off because none of us have one."

Alex made a face and dropped the dragon head back into her toolkit.

I reached into my own toolkit to see if I had anything that could help. I had some Potions of Healing, my diamond sword and a few other weapons. But if Dad's diamond pickaxe was no good, I didn't see how any of my items would be any better.

"We're going to need everyone as a group to break the crystals that give her health," Steve Alexander said. "That should take the health crystals out quickly. But that alone won't be anywhere near enough to stop her."

I tried to think. What would Maison say? We often came up with plans together, and she'd shown me tricks she'd learned on the *Minecraft* game that helped me in the Overworld. At the same time, I'd shown her tricks I knew in the Overworld that helped her with *Minecraft*. Our different levels of knowledge really complemented each other.

"Can you try to make another sword with the crystals you have?" Destiny asked.

Steve Alexander tried. The sword he managed to

make didn't even look like much of a sword. It was too short and it wasn't powerful enough. Frustrated, he broke the pieces up to think again.

"Can we use the shulker box to make something?" Alex asked.

"I've played around with those before," Steve Alexander said. "All they're really good for is keeping things in. The most you can do is dye them different colors."

What kind of a weapon would I make if I wanted to catch a dragon? I wondered. There were lots of different weapons in the Overworld: swords, spears, pickaxes, arrows. Even things like wooden blocks could be used as weapons in a pinch, though they didn't work as well.

Maison used to tell me one of her favorite things about *Minecraft* was that you could create basically whatever you wanted in it. You didn't have to follow a certain set of rules most of the time.

A sword had forced the Ender Dragon into the End, but that was it. It hadn't saved Steve Alexander from capture or prevented the Ender Dragon from escaping again.

There was also how dangerous these crystal pieces could be if they were turned into a weapon. Steve Alexander had kept warning us in his book that if a weapon made from these crystals fell into the wrong hands, they could be used for the ultimate destruction. That's why the Ender Dragon couldn't have them.

But what if there were other bad guys down the line, and they got their hands on the weapon we created? Should a weapon that dangerous really exist? Wouldn't everyone want it?

I remembered what the Ender Dragon had said when she'd turned against Steve Alexander: "If we do not take power, someone else will take the power from us."

We had to stop the Ender Dragon, there was no doubt about that. But what if others kept trying to take this power? Was it the greed for power that turned the Ender Dragon bad? Everyone wants a say, no one wants to be pushed down. But when someone is so ruthless they'll do anything to be in charge and make others suffer, that's how we got to where we were then.

Thinking back, there was only one time that she had successfully been kept from hurting people . . .

"I think I know what we should make," I said. "And it's not a weapon."

CHAPTER 11

E WERE DRAWING EVEN CLOSER TO THE Ender Dragon, and I could feel it. I was at the front of the ship, directing Yancy where to steer. We passed by islands with roaming Endermen and more End cities. Down in the cabin, I could hear Steve Alexander working on the crystal shards, making what I'd suggested.

"I still need the final crystal shard to finish it," he'd said. "But if we can get the shard away from Jean when she's not looking, I can finish this right away and we'll be ready."

No one had argued with me about my idea. Dad had even complimented it, which really excited me. (Maybe it also made up for me embarrassing Dad with the shulker disaster earlier.) It had seemed like a great idea, though as we got closer to our fight, I began to doubt myself. Could we really pull this off?

A shudder ran through me. It wasn't much farther! "There she is!" I cried, pointing into the distance.

"Where?" Yancy leaned forward, squinting.

Destiny looked out into the distance too and said, "I can see some islands, but . . ."

"It's her," I said, feeling it in my gut. "On that second island over there, do you see the big purple shape?"

Alex had also rushed up to see, leaning over the front of the ship so far she almost slipped over. "I see purple shapes, but I can't imagine anyone can make out what they are from here."

I stayed firm. "It's her, I know it is. I think that's a tall building from an End city on the island in front of her. But that second island? That's definitely her, so that must be where Maison is."

Hearing all this, Steve Alexander came out from the cabin.

"Stevie says that's the Ender Dragon," Dad said, as if he had to speak for me. I was pretty sure Steve Alexander had already heard what I'd said.

"If he says it's so, he's right," Steve Alexander said, nodding. "Meanwhile, I did the best I could with the crystals." He held up what he'd made, letting us see. He was right—it was not quite finished. Still, it looked better than his makeshift sword and anything else he'd tried to create in the cabin.

I liked that Steve Alexander had sided with me, though I wasn't really sure why he'd done it. Before I could ask, he went on, "It's time to make up our strategy. First, Yancy, I want you to steer the ship over so that we go up to the first island. We'll use that island as a shield and Jean won't be able to see us from where she is."

"On it!" Yancy said, steering hard. The ship shifted in what looked like outer space, taking us toward the island.

"Next," Steve Alexander said, "I want everyone but Stevie to work on breaking the crystals."

Wait, everyone but Stevie? Why not me too? Here I'd thought Steve Alexander was starting to like me because he'd agreed with my crystal idea and trusted my gut about where the Ender Dragon was. Now it sounded like he didn't want me to even be part of this mission!

"Each one of you will take out a health crystal," he continued. "You'll see them floating on columns in a circle around her. She might come after one or two of you, but she won't be able to come after all of you all at once."

"I'll do anything you ask to get my daughter back," Maison's mom said. "How are we going to save her?"

"I was just getting to that," Steve Alexander said. "Stevie, I have a special mission for you."

My heart leapt. What was he thinking?

"I want you to get Maison away from Jean and grab the last crystal shard," he said.

Now my heart wasn't only leaping—it was pounding. "How am I supposed to do that?" My voice sounded like a squawk when it came out. It wasn't supposed to sound like a squawk—it should have sounded braver than that. But why was Steve Alexander giving me the most difficult mission? Breaking crystals I could do. This? I wasn't so sure.

"You will be doing this while the others break the health crystals," Steve Alexander explained. "We need to do this all at once. Maison must be away from Jean for her safety, and also because as long as Jean has Maison, Jean has an advantage over us. She can use your friend as a shield or a hostage. We don't want that."

I gulped. No, we didn't want that.

"Once Maison is in the clear and you get the crystal shard, get the shard to me," Steve Alexander said. "I'll use it to quickly finish the invention. By then the health crystals should have all been taken out, and we'll all go after Jean at once."

"I still don't understand," I said. This time I didn't sound like I was squawking—this time it sounded like I was trembling. Probably because I was. "I can't take on a dragon. How am I supposed to get in there, help Maison and snatch back the crystal shard?" It was like going straight into a den of monsters. I didn't see how I could get there and get back out safely!

"Oh, I thought it was obvious," Steve Alexander said. "Stevie, you found the elytra. You're going to fly into the island, battle Jean in the air, save your friend and the crystal shard all without ever touching the ground."

CHAPTER 12

"I CAN'T DO THAT!" I CRIED. "I'VE NEVER EVEN FLOWN before!"

"Technically, elytra don't fly," Steve Alexander said. "You have to jump off from someplace high and then glide. The wings will last for about seven minutes. If you land, you won't be able to get back into the air unless you find someplace high to jump off again."

That made it even worse!

"Now, wait just a minute," Dad said. "Stevie is right. He has no experience in this. You or I should take the elytra."

"I need to be ready to finish the crystal invention at a moment's notice," Steve Alexander said. "And if Jean sees me right away, she won't allow that to happen."

"Then let me do the gliding," Dad said.

"You don't have any practice with it, either," Steve

Alexander said. "You didn't even know what elytra were an hour ago."

Whoa, that made Dad mad! He couldn't argue it, though, because Steve Alexander was telling the truth. (And I don't think he wanted to fight with the Overworld's greatest hero, because even if Steve Alexander didn't consider himself a hero, Dad still thought of him as one.)

"None of us knew what elytra were before an hour ago," Dad finally snapped.

"I did," Yancy said.

"Me too," Destiny said. "From playing *Minecraft*."

"Here's what you do, Stevie," Yancy said. "When I'm gliding with elytra in the game, I find it's easier to stay in the air if you keep pulling up and down at forty-degree intervals."

"What?" I said, not following at all.

"You know how math works, right?" Yancy said. "You have to if you make all these buildings. Three hundred and sixty degrees is a circle. Half of that, one hundred and eighty degrees, is a straight line. So this is ninety degrees, half of that." He held his arm out, with his forearm and hand straight up. "See that?"

"Yeah," I said slowly.

"So half of that would be forty-five degrees, so it'd look like this." He folded his arm down to demonstrate. "So forty degrees would just be a little below that."

I was swimming with details. Dad had taught me about angles for building, but it was one thing to know angles and another to pull off angles while you're in the air and fighting a dragon. I was totally overwhelmed.

"I . . . I don't think I can do this," I said.

"I'll do it!" Alex offered brightly.

"No," Steve Alexander said. "I see you have a bow and arrows, and we need your archery talents to take out the health crystals. Stevie has special talents that are needed here. It's because of his connection to Jean."

"I don't think that's really a talent," I said weakly.

"You have seen inside of her heart in a way none of the others of us have," Steve Alexander said. "Even I have never seen inside her to the degree you have. The reason you have the connection to her is for multiple reasons. One, you have my blood in you."

"So do Alex and my dad," I said.

"Two," Steve Alexander went on. "You have been an Enderman multiple times. Each time was to save your friends, and each time allowed her to dig her claws deeper into you, so that you can hear her voice."

He looked at Alex, who was pouting. "You are a great warrior," he told her. "This strategy has nothing to do with your lack of skills, and a lot more to do with Jean's obsession with Stevie. Once she got into his head, she felt convinced she could turn him to her side. It has infuriated her that Stevie is his own person."

"Of course I am," I said. "I couldn't listen to her." I didn't want to say how many times it'd been really tempting to give in to the Ender Dragon.

"Well, then I'm going to shoot up the health crystals

and Ender Dragon with arrows," Alex decided, looking pleased with herself. "I'll show her."

"And you will do a magnificent job, I'm sure," Steve Alexander said. "Now, if you'll excuse us, Stevie and I need to talk privately."

CHAPTER 13

I WENT WITH STEVE ALEXANDER DOWN TO THE BOT-tom room of the ship. Ossie was there, having made the empty shulker shell into a cat bed. She was purring and looking comfortable. Wolf had also joined us, sitting on the floor and watching what we were up to.

I felt so nervous. What did Steve Alexander want? Why did we have to talk privately?

The elytra I found were right there in front of us, resting on one of the chests. Even though the wings looked as if they couldn't weigh much, I thought the pressure of taking them on would make my shoulders sink.

"Alex is a way better fighter than me," I started out. I would still be fine handing the wings over to her and letting her take care of that part of the fight.

"I told you, this is more about your connection to Jean," he said. "And your connection to Maison."

My stomach plummeted.

"My dad is a better fighter than me," I said.

"Likewise, your dad has no connection to Jean and no real connection to Maison," he said. "And unlike you, it seems to me as if he doesn't like to try new things. He has his way of doing things, but that won't work against a dragon."

"Maison's mom has a bigger connection to Maison than I do," I argued. "It's her mom! That's more important than a best friend, isn't it?"

"Maison's mom is not trained in combat, or in any battle skills from what I can see," Steve Alexander said. "The Earth people have clearly grown weak since Maya's time. Maya knew how to fight, forage, and protect herself. Do they not train their children in these ways anymore? I see some fighting skills in Maison, Yancy, and Destiny, just not in the mother."

"They learned from *Minecraft*, I guess," I said. Maison had told me her mom was an architect, which meant she worked in a building all day and drew drawings for buildings. Back in Maya's time, people didn't work in buildings and had a lot more dangers to protect themselves from.

"But like you said, Yancy and Destiny know how to fight," I went on, even though I knew I was losing ground here. "I know Destiny's kind of quiet, and Yancy is kind of loud, but that's just how they are. Destiny is really good with computers and she likes to read. And Yancy . . . well, I think he's saying all those stupid pirate things to try to lighten the mood, because we've been so tense . . ."

Steve Alexander was staring at me in a way that made me go silent. He looked so serious.

"You went straight for those wings after we got in the ship," he said. "Didn't you get them because you wanted to fly?"

"I . . . I . . ."

"I will teach you how to glide," Steve Alexander said. "I can tell you the techniques I learned."

"But . . . but . . ." I glanced at his back. "Your wings are broken!"

"I will talk you through it."

"I . . . I can't!" I finally wailed.

"And why not? You've done so many things."

I finally got to the worst of it: "What if I fail?"

What if I couldn't glide right? What if Maison stayed the Ender Dragon's hostage forever? There were so many things to possibly go wrong!

"Fear should never stop you," he said. "Fear stops too many people. Fear is what lets people follow Jean, even though deep inside themselves they must know what they're doing is harmful. So many people would rather be safe than stand up for themselves. We have to stand up for everyone in the Overworld, because you heard from those villagers what's being done to all the people. And we can't just stand up mindlessly, expecting change—we have to make a bold strategy, where we can see how to get the results we want."

"How do you do it?" I asked. "How do you stay brave, even when she betrayed you? Even when she captured you?"

"Because either I had to live with her destroying my world, or I had to do something about it."

I thought about the people who'd bowed to the Ender Dragon. The ones who'd given up right away. Even the ones who'd insisted she was a good leader. I had seen all that and more in Steve Alexander's enchanted book, when he'd let me see into the past.

"I chose you to do this part of the mission because you'd already chosen yourself for it, without even knowing," he said. "I once thought that Jean was my best friend, and I let myself be blinded to the clues about her. I didn't want to believe she could be bad. Maison is your best friend, and if the tables were turned and you were stuck with Jean, I bet she would be flying out onto that island to save you."

Those words really hit home. I could picture Maison leaping off a building, wings spread, coming to help me. Not because she had to. Because she wanted to. Because we were best friends. Because if we didn't have each other, who did we have?

"You're right," I said. "Tell me everything you know about flying."

And I put on the elytra.

CHAPTER 14

A FTER DOCKING ON THE FIRST ISLAND, I QUICKLY climbed the purple skyscraper on it, watching the land below me get farther and farther away. The End ship looked small now. If I fell . . . no, don't think about it.

I pulled myself to the very top of the skyscraper and slid across it on my belly. On the island in front of me I could see the Ender Dragon sprawled out, her purple eyes glowing. A number of Endermen were on the island with her, as if they were standing guard.

That wasn't all I saw. Just like Steve Alexander said, there was a circle of obsidian columns looped around the island, and on top of each one was a health Ender crystal. These were bigger than the crystal shards we'd been finding, and they were all shaped like cubes. Two squares that looked like glass windows were over them, and the crystals were gently bopping up and down on top of the columns, as if they were in a soft breeze.

And there, in front of the Ender Dragon, was Maison.

Maison looked tiny from where I was kneeling, overshadowed by the massive dragon. She appeared grim and frustrated, but not scared or defeated.

Something glinted under the Ender Dragon's paw. It was the missing crystal shard! She was holding it under one huge foot as protection.

I looked to the side. After dropping me off on the first island, the ship was making its way to the Ender Dragon's island. I was told to wait until they were almost there, then attack. This distraction would allow them to get on the island and go after the health crystals.

The Ender Dragon was lounging like a happy cat after a special fish dinner, gloating. "It's taking them awhile, don't you think?" she asked Maison, as if wanting to rub it in.

"They're coming," Maison said, confident.

"Oh, I know they are," the Ender Dragon said. "It's amazing how well you can manipulate people over someone they care about. Right now I suppose they might be looking at all the destruction I've already caused."

"But we've been here this whole time," Maison argued.

"You think I can't rule from a distance?" the Ender

Dragon demanded. "I have my Endermen and mobs to take care of the dirty work. Even as we speak, they are turning all the people in the Overworld into my servants. And once everyone follows me, there will be no one to try to stop me. We're just waiting for your little friends to show up, so I can get the rest of the crystals. Then things will really get interesting."

"That's so like you," Maison said darkly. "To make others do your dirty work."

The Ender Dragon's eyes narrowed dangerously. "Watch your mouth," she said.

"Look at all these health crystals you have," Maison went on. "I don't think you're as strong as you act."

"You little—!" The Ender Dragon started to rise, then thought better of it. Forcing her voice low, she said, "You won't feel that way when I turn you into an Enderman."

"Stevie turned into an Enderman, and he never became your servant!" Maison said. "I won't, either! We're stronger than that! We can see through your lies!"

"Silence!" the Ender Dragon hissed.

"No!" Maison said. "You thought you'd bring me here and I'd be some scared little hostage who'd do whatever you want? Think again! Steve Alexander left us with the enchanted book and the guide to the crystal shards because he knew there would always be a way to defeat you!"

"Don't mention him!" The Ender Dragon responded to his name as if she'd been burned: she jumped back and seethed. Even as she moved, I saw she kept the Ender crystal shard with her.

I watched as the ship made its way around and almost reached the island with the Ender Dragon. It was now or never.

I slowly rose to my feet, the winds whipping all around me. They almost knocked me over. It reminded me of the dizzy feeling I had on the ship earlier, when I'd looked down into the void. Then I'd pulled back and stayed away from it. Now I had to jump right down there.

I took a deep breath and plunged off the skyscraper.

CHAPTER 15

A T FIRST IT FELT LIKE I WAS FALLING. THEN THE wings jerked open and I felt myself get lifted up on wind currents. I was gliding rapidly through the air, heading right toward the Ender Dragon!

Maison's face broke into a huge smile when she saw me. The Ender Dragon caught sight of me at the same time. "You!" she growled. "Have you brought me my crystal shards?"

"You'll never have them!" I shouted, swooping down. I felt like I almost couldn't control my speed, and I had to hold on. Almost before I knew it I was right by the Ender Dragon, and I slashed out with my sword, hitting her directly in the face!

She emitted a roar of anger, turning red momentarily. That meant it was a perfect strike!

I turned my body and zinged out of her way, barely missing her large jaws as they crunched down, trying to bite me. Then I swung back around, dizzying her, and struck her on the back of the head. Another perfect hit! I was starting to get the hang of this gliding, even if I were still a little rough around the edges.

Out of the corner of my eye, I saw the ship docking at the island and everyone but Steve Alexander jumped off. Endermen went at them, ready for the attack, and were knocked back by Alex's arrows.

The Ender Dragon leapt to bite me again and I barely dodged her. Some of the feathers from my elytra caught in her mouth and she spat them out. I zipped off to the side, plummeting down to the island.

No, no, no! I tried pulling myself up at a forty degree angle, like Yancy said, and I felt myself start to lift back up in the air. Then I felt the full weight of the Ender Dragon strike me with her paw, sending me flying back to the skyscraper.

I hit against the wall, shaken from the blow. My free hand scrambled, grabbed onto a jagged edge on the skyscraper and held myself in place.

"Oh, so you want a fight?" the Ender Dragon taunted. "I'll give you a fight."

Beating her wings, she flew up into the air. As she did, I saw light from one of the health crystals blast out and wash over her. Just like that, she was healed up as if she'd never been attacked to begin with.

Two could play that game. Gasping, I reached into my toolkit and pulled out some milk. After a quick drink, I felt my health quickly return. The empty milk bottle fell all the way to the ground below and shattered.

Then I threw myself back off the building and was gliding again, rushing toward the dragon.

Meanwhile, the Ender Dragon had spotted Alex shooting her arrows at a health crystal, almost breaking it. The dragon shot a fireball toward Alex, only for Alex to throw herself into a roll and get out of the way. Back on her feet, my cousin ripped more arrows out, shooting them straight for the Ender Dragon.

The arrows hit in the shoulder. Furious, the Ender Dragon dropped back to the ground. "You're the excellent archer," she said. "I think it's time to put you out of commission." Closer to Alex now, she shot another fireball at her.

But the dragon was so caught up in attacking Alex that she didn't notice something else important. During this time Maison had run to Dad, gotten a weapon from him, and returned. Holding Dad's giant pickaxe above her head, she struck the Ender Dragon's foot with all her might.

The Ender Dragon yelped out and let go of the last crystal shard.

Yes! Before anything else could happen, I swooped down in low, striking the Ender Dragon again with my sword. She snarled and drew back.

"I told you I wouldn't be a scared little hostage!" Maison shouted, seizing the shard.

"Maison, give me the crystal!" I called.

Maison threw the crystal up into the air, using her best baseball pitcher's throw. The crystal landed right into my hand!

"No," the Ender Dragon seethed. She was standing on the ground, a little shaken, but mostly furious. She did not expect us to all come in like this. Now that she knew what we were doing, the fury in her looked as if it could blow like TNT.

I was flying away from her, heading back to the ship where I knew Steve Alexander was. I needed to get him the crystal!

Even as I was hurrying, the Ender Dragon was gathering her strength back together and rising to the skies. Another health crystal blasted light at her, healing all the wounds she'd just gotten. No wonder Steve Alexander said we couldn't defeat her unless we took out all the health crystals first!

I peeked back over my shoulder and saw she was beating her wings again, rising into the sky and going straight for me. A fireball came shooting out of her mouth and I dove down. The fireball struck the skyscraper and set it on fire. And I was headed right toward it!

I veered to the side, missing the fiery skyscraper. I'd pushed too hard, though, and I felt myself start to plummet again. When I'd had that levitation curse on me, all I wanted was to get back to ground, and now I knew if I landed, I'd lose all advantage I had.

I tried to push myself forty degrees upward, and it

wasn't easy. I caught sight of Alex destroying a health crystal, and Yancy taking down another one. But I wouldn't be able to stay away from the Ender Dragon in the time it'd take to destroy all her health crystals!

The Ender Dragon was closing in on me like an evil shadow and her paw swiped out again. Her attack knocked me upward, so that I went spinning straight up and would be ready to fall back down again. She probably did it so I'd have the farthest distance to fall, but I could use this. I pushed myself against the wind, getting myself angled differently. I was still going to fall, though this time I had control over my fall.

And so when I plunged back down, I didn't hit the island or lose control over my wings. I fell directly on the back of the Ender Dragon, the way Steve Alexander used to ride her into battle. One second I was in the air, and the next I felt an enormous scaly body under me.

I could see the ship from here. Not giving the Ender Dragon a chance to return to her senses, I lunged off her, using her body as a new starting point to get my wings back in order. Below me, I saw Dad and Destiny take out two health crystals.

"You can't fly for long!" the Ender Dragon roared. "Those aren't real wings, like mine! Eventually they will give out on you!"

I was speeding for the ship, the ground rushing all around me, the Ender Dragon back at my heels.

As soon as I got over the ship, I threw the crystal shard down into the cabin, where Steve Alexander was waiting. Then I turned back around, almost face-to-face with the Ender Dragon. Her purple eyes were the size of a shield I'd use. Her mouth was open, the fangs set to grab me.

I pulled up at forty degrees, just zinging over her face, feeling her breath against me but dodging her bite. When I was on top of her head, I struck again with my sword. In the distance, I saw Maison's mom take out another health crystal. In fact, all the health crystals had been taken out except for one, and Alex was going at it with her arrows.

"I'll help you, Alex!" I called, rushing toward the last health crystal. I landed on the tall obsidian column, barely balancing myself there because there was so little room. Then I lifted my sword and struck the health crystal, breaking it to pieces.

CHAPTER 16

"THIS IS STILL FAR FROM OVER," THE ENDER Dragon growled. "Even without my health crystals I'm as strong as ever!"

She was right. She didn't have the same healing ability like before, though she was in perfect health from her latest healing, and the rest of us were looking pretty tattered.

"Get her!" Maison shouted, raising the diamond pickaxe. The others went rushing for the Ender Dragon, but she leapt into the air, out of the reach of swords and pickaxes. Arrows could still get her, and I watched Alex take the lead, striking her with fistfuls of quickly launched arrows.

I jumped off the pillar, going back into the fray of battle. As it was, the Ender Dragon was trying to shoot Alex with purple fireballs and head for the ship, where she'd seen me throw the crystal shard. I couldn't let her get there before Steve Alexander was done!

"Come and get me!" I shouted at the Ender Dragon as I jumped and flew back at her. I remembered those were the words Steve Alexander had mocked her with before their epic battle so long ago.

And the Ender Dragon remembered it too. A crazed look came over her eyes. "You!" she growled. "You only say that because *he* did!"

"Say his name!" I hollered. "Steve Alexander! I know all about your past, and you can't turn me against him anymore! Even if he isn't perfect, he isn't a coward like you! He doesn't seek our power through greed! He's everything that you're not!"

I came at her with my sword, but she was too fast, knocking me clear back so that I almost hit the burning skyscraper again.

"He's done for, that's what you mean!" she said. "Hero, genius, whatever you want to call him, when we first met all I saw was a lost soul desperate for some positive attention. And when I last saw him, he was behind bars. In the cell I put him in."

She opened her mouth and shot another fireball at me. I dove below it, inches away.

"He tried the same fight you're trying now," she rumbled, "gliding around with elytra. And I'll do to you what I did to him. I'll clip your wings and throw you in a cage so that you're my pet. And then, Stevie, you will finally bow to me."

"Not so fast, Jean," said a voice.

CHAPTER 17

STEVE ALEXANDER STEPPED ONTO THE ISLAND. He no longer looked like the staggering ghost of a person. He had the walk and expression of a man on a mission, the same way he'd looked when he'd taken on the Ender Dragon so many centuries ago.

In his hand he held a special chain he'd just made, using all the crystal shards. The invention I'd suggested, because when he'd first met her, she'd been in crystal chains, and it was the only thing that had ever stopped her. It might be the only thing that would ever stop her.

For the first time during this battle, I saw true fear on the Ender Dragon's face. "How . . . how did you get here?"

"It doesn't matter," he said. "What matters is that I'm here. And that I'm going to finish this."

Her snout puckered back in a vicious smile. But there was still fear in her eyes. "Don't make me laugh. Finish it? You never could finish anything that mattered. And what do you call that thing you have? That's no weapon."

"No," he agreed. "You'd like it too much if I made it into a weapon. So would any other mob cruel enough to understand its potential power. I'm not going to use it as a weapon. I'm going to use it for protection, to protect the Overworld from you."

"You're lying," she said. "The real reason you didn't make a weapon is because you can't bear to make me vanish forever."

"Perhaps," he said. "There is a reason I had to leave my time and my world. There's also a reason these kids have been risking their lives journeying all over to get these crystals. Because no matter who you used to be or pretended to be, we know who you are now. And you must be stopped."

And then he ran for her!

We all did. Coming at her from the skies, I tried to beat her down with my sword, weakening her and knocking her to the ground. Alex was filling her with arrows, making the dragon turn red repeatedly. Without those health crystals, and with so many people attacking her, the Ender Dragon was weakening fast. She tried to fly up, and soon found her wings were too weak. Snarling at us, still shooting fireballs, she sank to the ground.

"My Endermen!" she called. "Help me!"

In that instant, ten Endermen were on the attack.

"I'll get them with my arrows!" Alex shouted, turning to them. The Endermen kept trying to teleport away, but most of the time they found themselves getting hit with her arrows anyway.

"Ah ha!" Alex said. "I've gotten practice with you Endermen! Feel the wrath of the best archer under twelve in the Overworld!"

"You foolish Endermen!" the Ender Dragon raged, seeing she wasn't getting anywhere with them. I glided down and landed on her back. She tried to buck me off, knocking me to her lower back, but I stayed on. Meanwhile, with her down on the ground like she was, everyone was able to reach her.

In all the fray, I saw Steve Alexander leap forward, his crystal-studded chain flashing. She hissed at him and threw a fireball he easily dodged. She was so weak now she could barely put up any sort of a real fight.

Steve Alexander knelt and snapped the chains onto her feet. She tried to bolt free and wasn't able because the chains held her firmly to the ground. A furious, helpless shriek erupted from her mouth.

"It's over, Jean," Steve Alexander said. "You should be grateful that we grant more mercy to you than you have given to us."

"What . . . what are you going to do with me?" she cried.

"You will always stay in these chains," he said. "The

people who chained you before didn't warn anyone of your evils, so I will, to make sure no one is ever foolish enough to free you again. You will be kept in an obsidian prison that you cannot blast through. I will guard you personally. And the Overworld will be at peace."

She sighed and shut her eyes, exhausted, unable to fight anymore. "I will never be rid of you, will I?"

"No, but I didn't do this alone," Steve Alexander said. "The Overworld Heroes task force was with me on every step of the way. You lied to them, messed with their minds, tried to make them your servants. Others fell to your ways, but they didn't."

I started to grin then. I couldn't help it. Was all this really over? The others were smiling too. Maison's mom came up and gave Maison a big, relieved hug.

I knelt down in front of the Ender Dragon's face. She didn't look so scary now. "I came up with the idea for the chains," I said.

"After all that I did to you, you were the one who offered mercy?" She looked at me in shock.

"I did it before to someone called TheVampireDragon555," I said. "And he turned into Yancy, one of my best friends. But he knew what real friendship was, not your fake stuff."

"Aye, aye!" Yancy said with a salute. Blue, who was sitting on his shoulder, gave a happy chirp.

The Ender Dragon stared at Yancy a moment, then slowly shut her eyes. It looked as if she needed to rest. "How very interesting," was all she could say.

"And you know what the best part is?" Alex asked.

"What?" I said, looking at the defeated dragon. "That we did all this together? That I got to try out my elytra?"

"Nope," Alex said, crossing her arms. "Because we still have time for dinner. I told you we'd get this done in time."

CHAPTER 18

T WAS MAISON'S BIRTHDAY THAT WEEKEND, AND WE were all over at Maison's house for the party. By we, I mean Alex, Yancy, Destiny, Dad, Aunt Alexandra, Maison's mom, and Steve Alexander. And the pets— Wolf, Ossie, and Blue. And Maison of course.

Steve Alexander was baffled by how much Earth had changed. He didn't care much for phones ("I understand using them to contact people, but don't you overuse them?" he'd asked Yancy), and he was overwhelmed by the Internet. At first he was suspicious of the pizza, cake, and ice cream at the party because he didn't know where they came from. But after we convinced him to try a bite, he kept asking for seconds. I guessed all that hard work made him extra hungry.

There was food for the pets too. Wolf and Ossie were helping themselves to fish, and Blue had a bowl full of seeds to eat. Yancy started playing music on his phone and Blue began dancing to it, the way parrots in the Overworld dance to jukebox music.

"Here, let me find some pirate music," Yancy said.

Destiny took his phone away from him. "It's Maison's birthday," she said. "Let Maison decide what music she wants."

"Avast ye!" Yancy said. "Give me back my phone! You lily-livered landlubbers have no appreciation for music!"

Blue chirped as if in agreement.

After Maison blew out the candles on her cake, we started opening presents. Yancy and Destiny both gave Maison some video games and books about them, which I could tell Maison really liked. Her mom gave her some *Minecraft* stuffed animals.

"They sure look cute," her mom said as Maison hugged the stuffed zombies and Endermen. "But I bought those before this last week. I don't think those things are so cute in real life."

"Aw, Mom," Maison said, though she was smiling.

"My turn to give a gift!" Alex said. Grinning, she handed a sea lantern. I knew she'd made that from one we'd gotten from the ocean monument.

"Now that's something you don't see every day!" Maison said, laughing. "I'll put it on my desk, next to my computer!"

"May I have another piece of cake?" Steve Alexander asked, holding out his plate. He'd scraped it clean of all crumbs and icing.

"Sure," Maison's mom said, taking the plate. "Would you like one or two scoops of ice cream with it?"

"Three?" Steve Alexander asked with a bashful smile.

When she handed him back a plate with a slice of cake and *four* scoops of ice cream, he was all grins.

"I think we need to figure out how to make ice cream in the Overworld," Aunt Alexandra mused, polishing off the food on her plate.

"We don't have a way to keep it cold," Dad said.

Steve Alexander's eyes sparkled. "Not yet. But maybe I can figure out a way."

"Your newest invention is going to be about ice cream?" Alex said.

"It's been so long since I've been able to invent," Steve Alexander said. "I'm looking forward to it again."

These days Steve Alexander had moved in with Dad and me. After we'd chained up Jean, the Overworld and the End returned to being their own realms, and he'd created the obsidian prison he'd promised to keep the Ender Dragon in. Villagers from all across the Overworld had brought their supplies of obsidian so there would be enough. He still called the dragon Jean, despite everything. I wondered if she'd ever change or if she'd always be a dangerous mob who had to be locked up.

Steve Alexander promised to move out of our house, but Dad said he was welcome to stay as long as he wanted. I kind of enjoyed having him in the house. He was teaching me all sorts of new things about the Overworld, and I bet he enjoyed getting a new family with us. It was unreal having a legendary hero living in the same house as you. Sometimes he forgot to put books back exactly where Dad wanted them or he made a new meal in the kitchen so that we could smell it from wherever we were in the house. Normally Dad didn't like anything out of order, but he had a hard time telling Steve Alexander what to do.

"If we beat the Ender Dragon and get an Overworld ice cream maker all in the same week, I'd call that a success," Aunt Alexandra said. "Eh, Steve?" She nudged Dad.

Dad mumbled something.

"What was that?" Aunt Alexandra said, putting her hand to her ear as if she were having trouble hearing him. "Because you do remember whose idea it was to start this whole Overworld Heroes task force, don't you?"

Dad mumbled something else.

"He remembers," Aunt Alexandra said with a proud nod. Dad had been against it at the start and had fought the idea a lot of the way. Now it all had worked out, and he didn't want to admit he might have been wrong.

That was okay. I knew Dad's mumbling meant he was admitting something!

"It's time for Stevie to give his gift," Maison's mom said.

That pulled me out of my thoughts. My turn! I looked at Maison, who was smiling and eager for her gift. I was a little hesitant. I'd wanted to make her something unique, to let her know she was special to me. After all, before Maison, I'd never had a best friend.

"Here," I said, holding out a big, square box.

"Is that . . . a shulker box?" Alex asked, peering at it.

"Yeah, that's what I wrapped it in," I explained. Alex hadn't wrapped her gift, but Yancy and Destiny had wrapped theirs. I knew there was supposed to be some kind of a surprise around birthday gifts.

Maison gently took the shulker box and opened it. She gasped when she saw what was there.

"I hope you like it," I said, feeling bashful.

"Stevie, where did you find another pair of elytra?" Maison cried, lifting the wings out of the shulker box. She set the box to the side and Ossie climbed in, claiming it again as her new bed.

I looked down, not sure what to say.

"These are yours!" Maison exclaimed, realizing. "Stevie, I can't take these from you!"

"But I want you to have them," I said, pulling my eyes back up. "Because when I was flying, I realized something. The first time I got a friend, it was like getting wings. The whole world opens up to you."

Maison put her hand to her face, looking overcome. She didn't know what to say!

Someone clapped a hand on my shoulder. I turned, and there was Steve Alexander.

"Stevie, that's a beautiful gift," he said. "I know I really put you on the spot back there, having you do all the gliding while we fought Jean. So there's something I want you to have."

He reached into his toolkit and pulled out another pair of elytra.

"Where did you get those?" Now I was totally stumped.

"These are mine," he said. "I put them on an anvil and added leather to fix them as good as new. This way Maison can have a pair of wings, and so can you."

"But why would you give me these?" I sputtered.

"Because let's say that by freeing me, you gave me wings," he said. "Besides, I want to do more investigating and playing around with designs. Maybe I can design myself a flying potion or something. The sky's the limit!"

I took his elytra, still stunned.

"Hey, I want to go flying, too," Alex said.

"Yeah, I can be a pirate of the skies," Yancy said.

"Stop it with the pirates," Destiny said.

"I can share my wings," I said. "We can all take turns."

"Yeah, I'll share my wings, too," Maison said. She glanced sideways at a purring Ossie. "And I think Ossie should keep the shulker box. She's claimed it."

I laughed. "Okay! Did you hear that, Ossie? You get to keep that box!"

Ossie lifted her head and gave me an of-course-I-can-keep-it cat look. Then she put her head back down and went to sleep.

"Who's ready to try these out?" Maison asked eagerly.

"Ooo, ooo, ooo!" Yancy said, jumping up and down. Destiny beamed and Alex said, "Totally!"

"You kids go have fun," Maison's mom said. "You've earned it."

Laughing, we all ran to the portal to take us back to the Overworld. Our parents and Steve Alexander came with us. Maison and I climbed to the top of the tallest tree by our home, looking around at the sunshiny sky and the emerald green grass. It felt so good for the Overworld to be back to normal. To know that the Ender Dragon had been taken care of. To be back with my friends again, and know we were all safe and sound.

"Ready?" I asked Maison.

"I'm always ready," she said.

And we dove into the skies, flying together.

Special thanks to James Fitzgerald, Krishan Trotman and Rachel Stark, Jeremy Bonebreak, Dalton, Tobias and Rin, Eileen Robinson, Dan Woren, Alexis Tirado, Caitlin Abber, Andrea Johnson, Deborah Peckham and Peter Davidson, and Taylor Hite.

WANT MORE OF STEVIE AND HIS FRIENDS?

Read the Unofficial Overworld Adventure series!

Escape from the Overworld
DANICA DAVIDSON

Attack on the Overworld
DANICA DAVIDSON

The Rise of Herobrine
DANICA DAVIDSON

Down into the Nether
DANICA DAVIDSON

The Armies of Herobrine
DANICA DAVIDSON

Battle with the Wither
DANICA DAVIDSON

Available wherever books are sold!

CAN'T GET ENOUGH OF STEVIE'S ADVENTURES?

Remember, the entire Unofficial Overworld Adventure series is available as one great box set!

Available wherever books are sold!

DO YOU LIKE FICTION FOR MINECRAFTERS?

Read the rest of the Unofficial Overworld Heroes adventure series to find out what happens to Stevie and the Overworld Heroes!

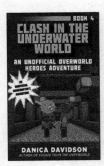

Adventure Against the Endermen
Danica Davidson

Mysteries of the Overworld
Danica Davidson

Danger in the Jungle Temple
Danica Davidson

Clash in the Underwater World
Danica Davidson

The Last of the Ender Crystal
Danica Davidson

Return of the Ender Dragon
Danica Davidson

Available wherever books are sold!

WANT EVEN MORE FICTION FOR MINECRAFTERS?

You can read the entire Unofficial Overworld Heroes Adventure series in a single box set, too!